To my mom and dad,
Thank you for believing in this adventure called Blue.

To my sweet wife,
There is no one I would rather share an adventure with.

And to my children, Gunnar and Tegan,
You are the greatest adventure of my life.

www.mascotbooks.com

Blue's Road Trip Through Indiana

For more information, please contact:
Mascot Books
560 Herndon Parkway #120
Herndon, VA 20170
info@mascotbooks.com

CPSIA Code: PRT0216A
ISBN-13: 978-1-63177-336-5

Printed in the United States

Blue's
ROAD TRIP THROUGH
INDIANA

by **Trey Mock**
Illustrated by **YOKO MATSUOKA**

The Indianapolis Colts play football and Blue is their biggest fan.
But when the team is off the field, Blue packs up his van.

You're invited to see the state, so grab a map and hop inside!
Explore Indiana A through Z, Blue will be your guide.

A Amish Acres

We're headed north on our first drive.
Amish Acres is where we arrive.

Delicious foods and crafts for sale.
Let's ride a buggy on Heritage Trail.

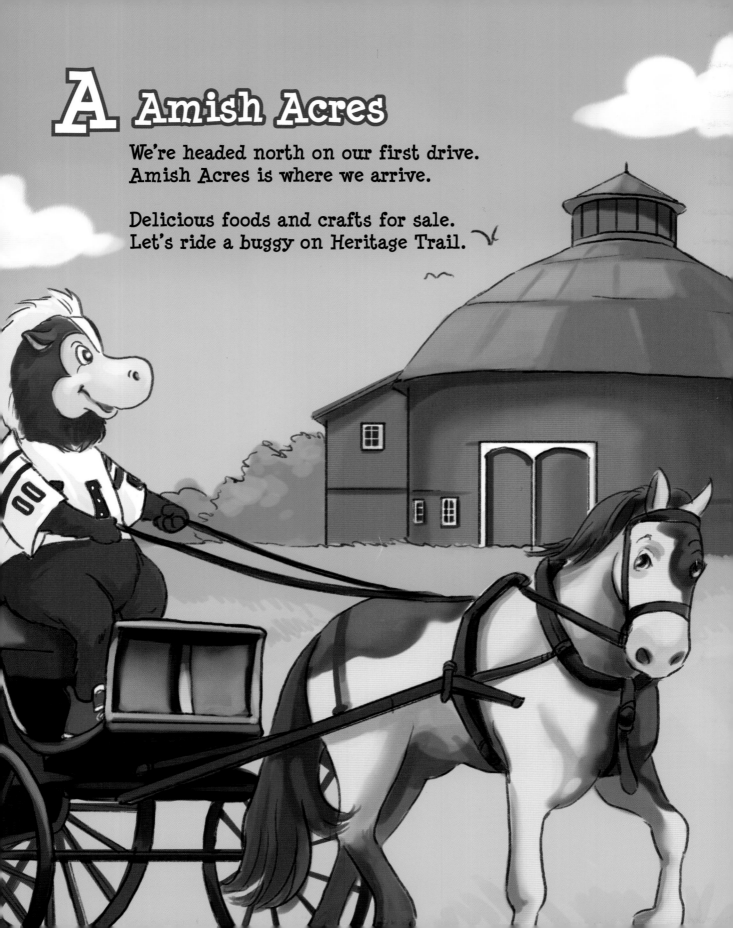

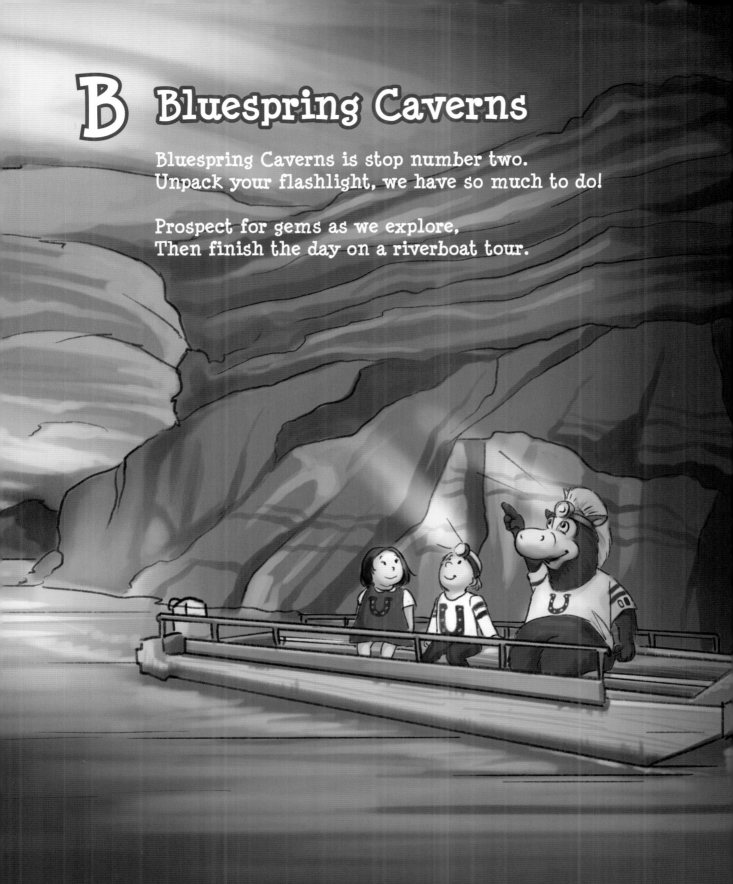

B Bluespring Caverns

Bluespring Caverns is stop number two.
Unpack your flashlight, we have so much to do!

Prospect for gems as we explore,
Then finish the day on a riverboat tour.

C Conner Prairie

To Conner Prairie where dreams take flight.
Up, up and away just like a kite.

Take a tethered balloon ride into the sky.
Then go exploring after you fly.

D Dairy Farm

To Fair Oaks Farms for our next thrill.
We can climb and jump in the town of Mooville.

See the miracle of a cow giving birth.
It's surely the best dairy farm on earth!

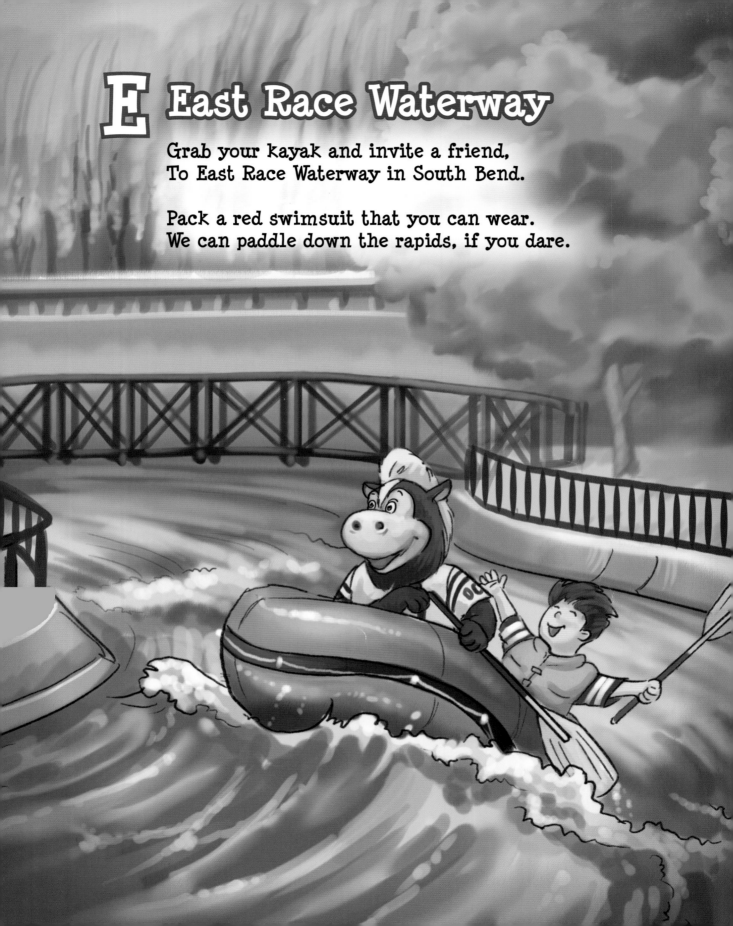

E East Race Waterway

Grab your kayak and invite a friend,
To East Race Waterway in South Bend.

Pack a red swimsuit that you can wear.
We can paddle down the rapids, if you dare.

F The Fieldhouse

Let's go to the Fieldhouse for a show.
Or cheer on our team against their foe.

No matter who plays, it's all the same.
We cheer for Indiana to win the game!

G Grissom Air Museum

Grissom Air Museum is the place to go.
If you like aviation, there's a lot you should know.

Learn about the planes that used to fly,
And the brave men and women who protect our sky.

Holiday World and Splashin' Safari

Let's head to Santa Claus. You really won't be sorry.
Welcome to Holiday World and Splashin' Safari!

The rides turn, dip, and twist as you swoosh down.
We can play all day in this happy little town!

I Indianapolis

Indianapolis has a nickname. We call it the "Circle City".
It's home to your friend Blue and is really quite pretty.

Indy is a nice place to live and the capital of our state.
The buildings are grand but the people make it great.

 Jasper

In Jasper, Indiana, there is an awesome train.
It's also where Lincoln went to grind his grain.

All aboard the Spirit of Jasper, to dine upon the tracks.
Then we can visit the City Mill to sit down and relax.

K Kosciusko County

Want to swim and ski all day?
Kosciusko County is the place to stay.

Over 100 lakes for your boat,
Or drift along on your float.

L Lucas Oil Stadium

Lucas Oil Stadium is Blue's favorite place of all.
It's where you can watch the Colts play football.

Find your seat and help Blue cheer for every play.
When we score the winning drive we'll all shout "Hooray!"

M Museums of Indiana

CHILDREN'S MUSEUM

Let's make a stop to pick up Liam.
On our way to a great museum.

Bring the whole family. You really should go!
Museums are a place for young minds to grow.

N Northern Dunes

Roll down the windows and turn up the tunes.
Let's head up north to Indiana Dunes.

We'll play on the beach and soak up the sun.
Surfing and swimming will surely be fun!

◯ Orange County

Orange County is a great place to be,
For the best golf and resort to ski.

Hit the links in the town of French Lick,
Or Paoli Peaks to try your best trick.

P Pokagon State Park

In the winter when the snow starts to fall,
We'll go to Pokagon State Park to have a ball.

Cross country skiing and fishing are fun,
But nothing beats sledding the Toboggan Run.

Q Quilt Gardens

Every year when spring begins to start,
The Quilt Gardens turn flowers into art.

Beautiful patterns will grow from the ground.
But when it gets cold, the flowers can't be found.

R Racing Capital of the World

Let's head to Indy at the end of May
To see the race at the Motor Speedway.

The Racing Capital of the World is a blast.
Watch drivers as they race really fast!

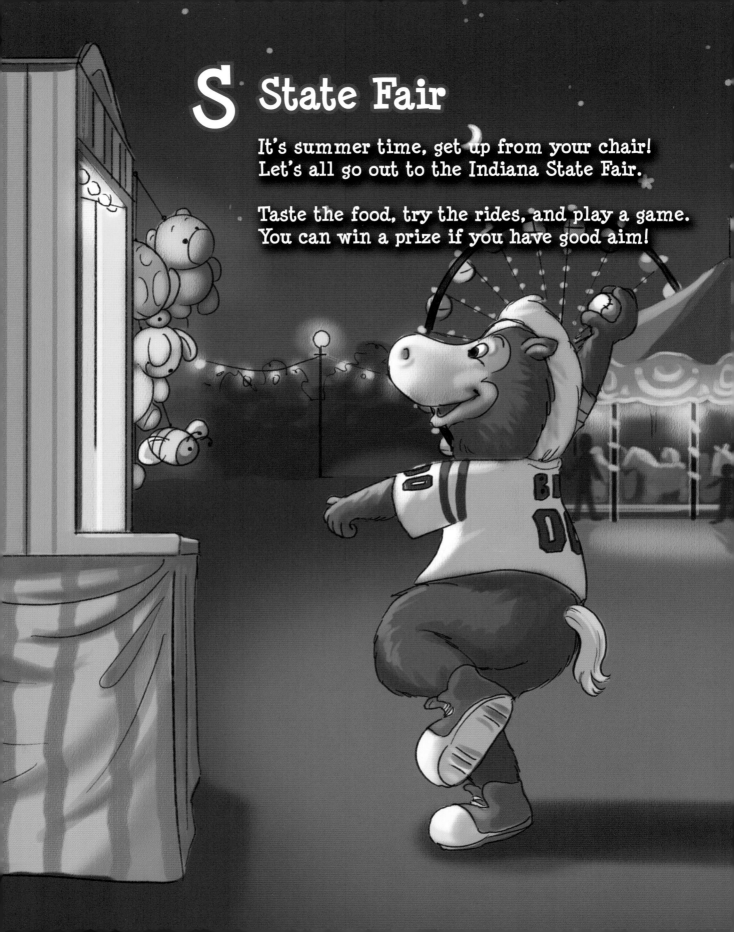

S State Fair

It's summer time, get up from your chair!
Let's all go out to the Indiana State Fair.

Taste the food, try the rides, and play a game.
You can win a prize if you have good aim!

T Turkey Run State Park

The sun is setting. It's getting dark.
Set up the tent at Turkey Run State Park.

Wake up in the morning and hike a peak.
Then paddle your canoe down Sugar Creek.

U Universities

If you want to grow up and have a job that's cool,
A university or college is where you should go to school.

You can be anything in the world that you want to be.
But you'll need a good education; it is the biggest key.

V Victory Field

Let's go to a ball game. Come on, grab your glove!
Victory Field is home to a game we all love.

When our team's up to bat, we'll cheer for each run.
The Indianapolis Indians are always number one.

W War Memorial and Soldiers and Sailors Monument

The War Memorial honors those who fought for you and me.
It's because of these brave men and women that you and I are free.

Climb the Soldiers and Sailors Monument to see Indy from above,
It's at the center of the city with a view that you will love!

X X Marks the Spot

X marks the spot where trains used to ride the rail.
Now we can play up and down the Monon Trail.

Grab your bike or go for a jog.
It's a wonderful place to walk your dog.

Y Yogi Bear's Jellystone Park

Yogi Bear's Jellystone Park makes camping great.
They aren't hard to find, there are seven in our state.

Set up camp, take a hike, there's always something to do.
For lunch we'll have a picnic with Yogi, Cindy, and Boo Boo.

Z Indianapolis Zoo

Check out all the animals at the Indianapolis Zoo.
We'll see a polar bear, tigers, and cheetahs too!

You can see a dolphin swim, if you get the chance.
Watch an elephant paint or a penguin do a dance.

BLUE

Our journey is finally over. This book is finally done.
But your adventures don't end here, go out and have some fun!

Tear Blue out and pack a bag. There's still so much to see.
The world is waiting for you, go explore it A to Z.

Cut out this picture of Blue and take him on
your next adventure. Then, take a picture and
send it to Blue on social media!

Please post your picture using #roadtripwithblue

About the Author

Trey Mock is entering his eleventh season as the "man behind Blue". He started his mascot career as Aubie at Auburn University. In 2006, he created Blue for the Indianapolis Colts. Trey and his wife Ali Mock reside in Westfield, Indiana with their son Gunnar and daughter Tegan.